The Adventures of
Jack & Adam

The Widow

Anthony Broderick

Copyright © Anthony Broderick, 2017
First Published in Ireland, in 2017, in co-operation with
Choice Publishing, Drogheda, County Louth, Republic of Ireland.
www.choicepublishing.ie

Paperback ISBN: 978-1-911131-21-2
eBook ISBN: 978-1 911131-88-5

eBook ISBN: 978-1-911131-87-8 The Larry Right Series Episode 2

This book is a work of fiction. All characters in this book are fictitious,
and any resemblance to actual persons, living or dead, is purely
coincidental. Names, characters, places or incidents are a product of
the author's imagination and are used fictitiously.

A CIP catalogue record for this book is available from
the National Library.

Introduction

Halloween is approaching and the boys have come to the conclusion of yet another school term. A lot has been learned by Jack and Adam over the past few weeks and they look forward to spending a normal Halloween night in their local neighbourhood. However things take a twist before and during the night that leave the boys in a state of trauma. While they feel happy and secure in their bountiful environment, they unearth a new found respect for someone who has always been central to them.

Chapter 1 – Money Well Spent

"I hope this Halloween is as good as last year's," said Adam, waving his legs back and forth. He was sitting on the wall awaiting the arrival of the school bus.

"Yeah, it will be hard top that fireworks display. But I have a few things up my sleeve," replied Jack with a smile. He knew that at this time of year his wild antics had more of a chance of being tolerated.

"We'll have to check out the Hidden House this year. There could be someone living there now," he added.

"We can do all of that as long as you keep your act together at school," answered Adam. He threw a sharp glance in his brother's direction.

Jack's behaviour in school had improved greatly after an incident that took place during the first week of term. For some strange reason he had escaped from school on the Friday evening by opening the emergency exit at the back of the new fifth-class prefab. Mr Atkinson, who had moved up to teach fifth class, to Jack's dismay, had no choice but to set down a firm marker and suspend him for three days. Mum and Dad were furious as they hoped he would have grown up a little, now that he was approaching ten years of age. Adam, on the other hand, had made a reasonable start to his new academic year. Although he nearly died of shock when he found out that Mr Atkinson would be his teacher for a second consecutive year, he was doing his utmost to focus from the start and not fall behind in any subject.

Break time at school was very different during the autumn. The pupils wrapped up warm in their hats and coats before venturing out into the sharp air. Icy cobwebs hung from bushes around the school playground, and some younger children ran around breathing out heavily as if they were smoking cigars. Adam found it strangely comforting to come back into the warm classroom after breaks as the cold outside was sometimes numbing.

Mr Atkinson had informed the class that they

would be allowed to wear a Halloween costume, or just a mask if they chose, into school on the day before the school break. He had been in a good mood since becoming a father for the third time three weeks ago. Jack had noticed a picture of his new-born on the screen of the phone on his desk when he went up to present his homework one morning. He knew this was probably the reason for Mr Atkinson's pleasant mood swing.

He was even allowing the class to do some art in the days running up to October 31st. Adam had painted an image of Satellite Stan with his mini computers attached to his leather technician's belt. Jack had tried to make his own Halloween mask, painting a plastic plate white with three holes cut out for a pair of eyes and a mouth. He went around the classroom pretending he was a vengeful ghost, but most students just laughed. They thought he looked more like a mime artist.

In the run up to the holidays, all the sixth class were constantly chatting about a big Halloween party that Harry Fog was having at his house. It was really Harry's brother, William, a second-year secondary school student, who was organising it. Many of Jack and Adam's classmates were allowed go to it but the brothers were told by their parents that they had to spend Halloween night in their own village. Adam envied all the boys and girls who were going, as William had given an open invite, allowing anyone from nearby to come, and it was undoubtedly going to be the place to be on October 31st.

At home Mum had gotten into the festive mood and had decorated the hall with gory skeletons and beside the front door there were some hollow skulls that lit up. Granny had brought over two big tarts and inside there was a whole variety of treats, from rings to miraculous medals to money. Everyone in the house wanted to get the two euro coins. They were wrapped in cling film and hidden inside some of the slices. Outside Club stretched up onto the kitchen window to see what was going on. She would have settled for a bit of the crust. Diamond pawed at the door, eager to come inside.

"Come on in, you," said Dad. He opened the back door and allowed Diamond to come in out of the cold and rest in front of the hot range. Diamond scampered in and leaped straight into her basket after hearing a loud bang from just across the hedge.

"She can stay in for the evening. She's getting a bit frightened outside with all those noises," said Mum. She understood that Halloween could be a dangerous time for animals, especially cats. She remembered from last year how both Club and Diamond had endured an hour or two of trauma. There had been loud noises coming from the woods and both animals had spent the time darting from side to side and shaking in fear as if their nerves had gone. It had been difficult to watch. Dad had even taken a radio from inside and turned it up loudly in the garden to distract their attention from the explosions and reduce some of their fear.

Did you get the pumpkins?" Adam asked eagerly as he took off his uniform.

"Yes, they're beside the fridge," answered Mum. She pointed over her shoulder at her big bag of shopping.

Adam quickly put on some casual clothes and began experimenting with one of the pumpkins.

Jack was often puzzled at how much his brother enjoyed sticking his hands in amongst the slime and seeds of the pumpkins and pulling out the insides.

"That really is sick, and the smell is disgusting!" commented Jack. He gulped down a few monkey nuts and piled their empty shells on the table.

"Says the guy who's eating more than his weight in nuts," replied Adam as he set about cutting out slots in the pumpkin to form the nose and mouth.

"Can we go to the auction tonight, Dad?" asked Jack, realising that it was Wednesday and all the good gadgets and masks would be on offer.

"If all the homework is done you can come with me so," answered Dad. He frowned at Jack to point out that he really meant it when he said "all homework done".

Jack raced to his room to begin some English.

He did not want to miss out on his Dad's regular trip to the auction. The two boys looked forward to strolling around from stall to stall, observing the different Halloween costumes and strange gadgets for pranking people with that were often on sale at the auction before Halloween. Jack remembered from last year that you had to be early to get the good stuff.

The auction was held on the outskirts of Willows Town. It was an area where lots of people lived and was a very peaceful part of the country. A form of market took place for the first few hours each Wednesday evening before vehicles like tractors and cars were auctioned off later on in the night, which was how the event got its name.

Rory, a pupil from a nearby school, lived out there. He often helped his father at the gates, letting people in and out and showing them where to park. He would sometimes brag about making loads of money on tips from some of the wealthy farmers, but really the boys knew he was talking absolute rubbish. Adam knew Rory from playing opposite him on the football field. Rory always made it his business to chat to Adam after each game and in many ways wanted to become his friend. Adam tolerated Rory, unlike others. Very few people wanted much to do with Rory because of the bad reputation that he had created for himself over the years.

It was very cold and muddy at the auction, as it was held in a marshy equestrian centre where horses were trained. The boys wore their jackets and made sure to put on their wellingtons to avoid destroying their runners. Life at the auction almost brought you back in time to the Middle Ages. Different tradesmen, from tin smiths to jewellers, stood in front of their own individual stalls, shouting out their bargains, hoping to attract as many buyers as they could.

Jack quickly located the stall that was selling the Halloween masks and stared in with his mouth open. He scanned the different shelves in search of something he fancied.

"Which one would you like, young lad?" a man with a husky voice called out.

"Emmm, I think that's a good one!" answered Jack, pointing at a spooky-looking mask with long dangling grey hair attached at the top.

"Yes, that is a scary mask, very realistic," replied the heavy-set man. He reached over to take it off the stand.

He then placed it over his huge head and stared into Jack's young face. Jack was taken aback by how human the mask looked, and his eyes lit up in excitement.

'It's ten euro. I'll put it in a bag for you?" said the man, casually reaching for a plastic bag under the counter.

Jack paused for a moment to consider his options. He knew the men that sold at these stalls had all the selling tricks and felt this stall owner was desperate to get a sale.

"Ten euro, that's too much. I saw one at another stall that was a lot cheaper. I might take another look at it," answered Jack. He realised he could get it a lot cheaper if he acted cute and tried to haggle.

"How much do you have?" said the man, keen to hold Jack's interest.

Jack stood back and thought for a moment. He remembered that his Dad would always pretend that he only had a small amount of money with him to try and get the item as cheap as he could. Jack had fifteen euro. He shoved his hand into his left pocket where he had one of the five euro notes and pulled it slowly out.

"I just have five euro," replied Jack. He waved it in front of the stall-holder.

"Ah no, that's not enough, the mask is worth more than that!" said the man. He glanced up and down in search of more customers.

"Okay, that's no problem!" Jack quickly responded, placing his money back in his pocket. He turned in the direction of another stall just to his right. He casually walked towards it and then reached down again to his pocket, as if to take his money back out to purchase something on sale here.

As soon as he did so, he heard the man shouting from behind him.

"Ok, five euro and the mask is yours," he said reluctantly.

Jack stood still, and smiled wryly to himself before turning back to get his bargain of the night. His instinct had been correct. He knew that if he acted like he was going to spend his money elsewhere, the man would call him back. Now he had saved five euro and had gotten a fantastic Halloween mask. He popped it in a plastic bag and made his way to where Adam stood.

Adam was cautiously observing the gadgets and pranks on sale in the stall beside the entrance. He was really fascinated with the range of smoke bombs and eerie Halloween props that were on sale here. Even the owners of the stall had gotten into the Halloween spirit. A man and his wife had their faces painted very artistically. Adam could tell it was a man by the uncanny voice and large physical presence. He was obviously dressed up as a villain from a horror film. He had his face painted completely white with black around his eyes and a streak of red stretching across his face.

His wife, on the other hand, was dressed up as Lizzy Furnish, a new superhero that everyone was talking about. *Lizzy Furnish: The Movie* had been playing in local cinemas and it was undoubtedly going be a big hit as a Halloween costume also. Lizzy was a fascinating character. She was a young government agent who had the ability to change into any type of furniture. She used this power of morphing into tables, chairs, presses and wardrobes to overhear conversations and gain key pieces of information. The woman was dressed in Lizzy's usual attire, flowery shirt and walnut-coloured trousers, and had a fake mole on her left cheek just like Lizzy. It really did look well.

This stall had such a variety of Halloween products that the boys would have loved to have bought everything.

Adam also had fifteen euro and decided to buy a packet of smoke bombs that lit up red and yellow, along with a black cloak with skeleton bones drawn on it for Club. He laughed to himself as he handed in his money to pay for the two items.

On his way out, Adam noticed William Fog and two other teenagers carrying large brown bags tight to their waists. They moved briskly through the auction before disappearing out through a side door.

Jack wore the mask he had bought around the house all the time for the next day and wore it into school on the Friday, the day of their school holidays. He did not seem to mind the fact that it was very itchy to wear. He just enjoyed creeping up behind anyone he met and trying to frighten them out of their wits.

Chapter 2 – Plans Go Up in Smoke

There was a great buzz in school on the half-day before the break. Everyone was allowed to play Halloween games throughout the day and watch a movie at eleven o'clock. Adam felt strange wearing his mask, as for the first time he did not feel worried and anxious when approached by Mr Atkinson. Mr Atkinson could not tell who he was. It was almost as if he was a different person for the day and left his old fearful self at home. All the boys' friends had brought in packets of sweets for the day's activities and everyone was eating as much as they wanted. Jack had brought in a packet of his monkey nuts that kept him munching away until one o'clock.

Parents looked confused as they waited in their cars to collect their children from school. All of the pupils were still wearing their masks and the scene resembled one from a horror movie where all the zombies and monsters had come alive.

Mum was parked outside to collect the boys and had the heating on full blast in the car.

"Are you all ready to go trick-or-treating tonight, boys?" she inquired. She turned around and smiled at the two shivery Halloween faces.

"Dead right!" mumbled Jack.

"What time is Paul coming over?" asked Mum. Paul was Adam's best friend.

"He said he would be over around four," replied Adam, waving out of the car window to a few of his friends as they drove off.

"That's good. Well, if you want to invite any more friends like Paul you're more than welcome, it's a pleasure to have him in the house," said Mum.

"Sure they're all going to Fog's house," answered Adam in frustration. "Why can't we even go for a little while?"

"You'll have just as much fun at home. And wait until you see all the stuff I have bought in for later," answered Mum. She winked back at Jack through the rear-view mirror.

As soon as Jack got out of the car he began preparing the food for the evening, placing all the necessities on the table. There were a range of fizzy drinks, monkey nuts, sweets of all kind and even some Halloween brack. All of Granny's tarts had been polished off last night and it was Adam who was fortunate enough to have gotten the lucky slice containing the two-euro coin. Jack went about assembling some lucky bags for the trick-or-treaters who would come knocking later. In each bag was a fifty-cent coin along with a number of chocolate bars and sweets. Sometimes Mum packed in some fruit, but Jack knew that was the last thing children wanted to be eating on Halloween night.

Adam had set up different areas in the kitchen for Halloween games. In one area a basin of water along with an apple was left for the 'Bobbing for Apples' game. Beside the door a string hung from the roof with an apple tied on the end so they could play the 'Snap Apple' game where people tried to bite as much of the apple as they could without using their arms. The two customised Halloween pumpkins were laid out in front of the window and a creepy spider was left dangling from the knocker on the outside door. The place was really looking haunted and there was every prospect of a very enjoyable and fun-filled evening.

After the place was fully set up Adam and Jack raced outside to try out the new smoke bombs. Mum glanced out sometimes from the window to check on them, but she knew that these gadgets were relatively harmless. Jack flicked on the outside light and Adam carefully lit a match to ignite the end of one of the round, red smoke pellets. Adam made sure he was careful lighting the match and stood well back when the pellets were letting off the smoke. As the smoke bomb caught fire, the pellet began to release red vapour into the air. There was very little wind so the smoke lingered. Club cocked her ears. She sniffed the strange odour filtering out from the colourful fumes and listened to the singeing sound of the burning. Adam and Jack gazed in amazement as they took in this wonderful spectacle. Adam then lit another red smoke bomb, along with a bright yellow one. Placing them side by side, the colours mixed together, creating a magical sight.

Up into the night sky the smoke drifted, leaving behind a red and yellow stain on the black tarmacadam. "They're pretty good," said Adam, staring up into the sky.

"Yeah, but they don't last long, give me a few more," said Jack. He took three of the smoke pellets and walked up to the front gate.

Adam, unsure what he was up to, followed his brother as he walked through the gate and about twenty metres down the road. Lighting one of the red pellets and placing the other two on top of it, he dashed out onto the road when it was safe and positioned the pellets on the centre white line. Adam saw what his brother was up to and he really didn't approve. Jack ducked behind a wall and watched the smoke fill the air once again, this time with triple the effect, and it soon blocked out all sight of the main road.

He saw a car come down the road, and signalled for Adam to get down and hide beside him.

The brothers heard a car jamming on its brakes, the driver unable to see through the thick fog of red smoke. Jack had seen in cartoons before how the good guys would sometimes try and smoke out the bad guys by tossing a smoke bomb in through a window. He hoped the man driving the car would appreciate the humour of it all and just advance through it and continue on his way. Adam giggled as yet another car squeezed on the brakes to navigate around the thick mist. Although it was quite dangerous, he couldn't help admiring the wicked inventiveness of his brother's mind.

Before long the boys had had their fill of the smoke bombs, and Adam was just after witnessing ten euros' worth of his communion money drifting up into the still, pitch-dark night. But he felt it was worth it.

They were met by their mother as they re-entered the house. They could see the peculiar look on her face and got the feeling that something wasn't right.

"I thought you said you weren't inviting anyone over apart from Paul," said Mum, sounding puzzled.

"What do you mean, it is only Paul that's coming over," replied Adam. He leaned back onto the steel bar in front of the hot range.

"Well, some boy called Rory is just after

arriving, saying that he's coming trick-or-treating with you and Jack," said Mum, trying to keep her voice down.

There was a momentary pause as all parties tried to process the new information.

"What, Rory? I hope it's not Rory Phillips. He wasn't invited! And is he here?" asked Adam. He looked around in astonishment at his brother.

Jack puffed out a breath and made his feelings heard.

"That's awful cheek! You'd better sort this out, Adam. I don't want to go around with him!'

"Well, he's down in the sitting room now. Maybe on this occasion you can let him come round with the two of ye, there's no point in being rude," said Mum.

"Rude? You should see what he's like!" answered Jack. "There is a reason why nobody invites him to their house," he added under his breath.

"Listen, he's down watching TV now, just give him a chance. He seems quite nice," said Mum. She then crossed her hands and awaited a decision.

"Ha, if you knew what he did in the changing rooms last week you wouldn't be allowing him near the house," answered Jack.

Adam thought about it for a moment. Now that Rory was down in his sitting room it would be very difficult to just boot him out. Maybe he should give him a chance, he thought. He also didn't want his brother to continue raising his voice to Mum.

"OK, I'll go down to him now," said Adam. "Come on, Jack, it won't be that bad," he added.

Jack turned away in disgust. He clutched the packet of monkey nuts as if to ease the pain.

"He'd better be well behaved!" he said, ironically pointing his finger towards his mother.

Adam opened the kitchen door and walked down the hallway towards the sitting room. He could hear the television on and Rory laughing out loud. Adam pushed the door open.

"Heyyyyyy, Adam mate, how are ya? I was passing by and thought I'd pop in for the evening, I hope that's OK," said Rory confidently, getting up out of his seat.

Rory was dressed up as someone who had just

risen from the dead. He wore a white skull mask and had a skeleton costume covering the whole of his body. He really did look very intimidating, with his hollow eyes, sunken nose and pale white face.

"Yeah, Mum was telling me," replied Adam still somewhat in shock.

The gang were soon joined by their classmate, Paul. Paul was surprised to be greeted by Rory at the front door but was soon informed about what had happened.

They all started off playing the bobbing for apples game. Jack was the only boy to bite off a piece of the bright green apple, but Paul reckoned that he had forced it down to the bottom of the basin and then sunk his teeth in to grasp it. The game was enjoyable at first, but after a few attempts at grasping the apple using tongues and teeth, the basin of water needed to be changed. Rory was the main culprit. He sometimes swallowed gulps of water and then just spat it back into the basin.

"Let's do something different," Adam suggested, looking in disgust as Rory spat into the basin of water once again. He made his way over towards the apple dangling from the ceiling.

It was funny how all year they looked forward to playing these games and when they finally played them they got bored and fed up within minutes. It reminded Adam of the time his Dad had bought them a full-sized snooker table and put it together upstairs. It was a big job carrying the heavy plates of slate up all the steps, so Dad organised a few sturdy men from work to lend a hand. The table was beautifully laid out upstairs with a large light hanging overhead to bring out the outline of the table and illuminate the snooker balls. There was no full-sized snooker table in all of Willows Town, so having one in the house was greatly envied. Adam and Jack started off playing games morning and evening. They would bring friends over and sometimes on Fridays would play late into the night. But it wasn't long before they were only going upstairs to play if snooker was on the television, mainly around the time of the world championships. The table took up so much space that Dad had no other option than to sell it within a few months.

"I've had enough of this game as well. It's just too hard!" cried Adam, as the swinging apple smashed against his front teeth again.

"Yeah, this is very annoying!" said Jack with a look of disgust on his face. "What else can we do?" he asked impatiently, just like Adam had minutes beforehand.

Just then they heard a loud knock on the door, soon followed by another one. Adam felt a strange sensation making its way up his spine as he thought about who it might be. But then he felt silly. It was Halloween, so it was probably just early trick-or-treaters. Jack grabbed a few of the prepared goody bags and handed them to his Mum, who distributed them to the young revellers.

"Come on, Adam, we can't let these strangers come into our village and get all the treats. We have to get ready and go out before it gets too late," Jack ordered, then rushed up to his room for his gear.

Adam signalled to the others that his brother was right and he too grabbed his Halloween mask and the other accessories he had left on a nearby chair.

When all team members were ready, they met at the front gate and had a brief discussion about their plans for the night. The evening was quite cold but that wasn't going to stop the crew getting as many sweets, money or other surprises as they could get their hands on. The other trick-or-treaters had disappeared into the distance so it appeared to be just them out for the time being.

Adam wore one of his Dad's big old black coats. His aim was to try and make himself look as big and unfamiliar as possible, wearing layer upon layer. He wore the mask he had bought three years ago that looked like an evil goblin. He always found this mask very convenient as it was easy to put on and take off and relatively comfortable to wear.

Dad placed the skeleton costume over Club and nudged her out the door. Unusually, Club was hesitant to leave the warm house, with all the treats of food displayed inside. Dad realised that she would probably be recognised by most of the neighbours and thus blow the boys' cover, but he also felt that she provided some protection for the group of boys on their own at this time of the evening.

Adam decided that splitting up into groups of two would be the best ploy. The idea was that they could cover a vast area in less time that way. If people saw four trick-or-treaters at the door they would probably give them one bag of goodies between them, instead of one each.

"I'll go with Paul!" shouted Jack, for fear he would get partnered with Rory.

Adam threw a sharp glance at Jack, out through the mask's goblin eyes, and then turned to Rory and gestured that he follow him the opposite way.

The local area was mostly familiar to Jack and Adam, and even though they didn't know the exact names of some of the people in the houses, they still knew the type of people they were and the best things to say to them to maximise profits.

Chapter 3 – Rory's Bad Manners

Adam and Rory headed along the opposite side of the road to the others, with Club following closely behind. Her two black eyes really stood out from the contrasting white skeleton cloak hanging from her sides. Deciding to give the Dots' house a miss for obvious reasons, the boys approached their first target. It was a young couple's house and Adam felt that they would be quite generous with treats. The house was brightly lit and smoke was puffing rapidly from the chimney. Rory reached for the doorbell and pushed the small white button aggressively. Adam found it a little nerve-wracking as he waited for the couple to come to the door. He felt a little surge of blood through his veins; he hoped he would not be recognised underneath the mask.

"Trick or treat! Trick or treat! Can we have something nice to eat?" Adam mumbled politely as a couple arrived at the door. Rory was just uttering "*Give* us something nice to eat!!" in his abrupt tone, but Adam tried to cover it up by talking louder. The man and his wife took a good look at the two boys and complimented them on the originality of their costumes.

"So where did you two come from?" asked the woman as she waited for her husband to come back to the door with some sweets.

"Make sure you give us some money," muttered Rory in a sarcastic tone under his mask.

"We came from town," replied Adam. He gave Rory a nudge, annoyed at his ignorance.

The woman had heard what Rory said. She nodded her head and waited in silence for her husband to return.

When the man came back with the bag of treats, Club went forward and began jumping up to get some of the food.

"Get down! Get down, Club!" Adam screeched. He was panicking slightly at this stage as he knew he shouldn't have called her by her proper name. Rory grabbed the plastic bag and raced out to the next house.

"Thanks!" said Adam, embarrassed. He prayed

the couple didn't recognise his voice and think that he was with his brother, Jack. Club, realising that Rory was off with the bag of food towards the next house, sped down the steps and followed him along, eagerly awaiting a sweet or two to be thrown on the ground.

"I think Club is holding us back!" said Rory. Impatiently he kicked a gate open to enter another driveway.

Adam felt he was just making excuses. He also felt Rory would need to change his tone when addressing the locals to have any future success. They covered the next five houses along the village until they came to the end of the street. Adam did all of the talking, while Rory was happy enough to take credit for the full bag of sweets and coins in his hand.

At the bottom of the street the boys and Club walked into the small gateway of a grey detached house. Adam wasn't too sure who lived here but knew he would probably recognise them when they came to the door. There was a light on in one of the rooms and smoke made its way out from the chimney. Adam reached for the door handle while Rory and Club panted heavily into the cold air, waiting for the door to open.

Adam sensed no movement inside the house. He knocked again, a little harder, but still nobody came to answer. Rory pulled his hands out from underneath his costume and thumped his fist on the handle.

"What are you doing? You can't do that!" shouted Adam, furious that Rory had been so disrespectful. Even Club could sense the frustration in Adam as she tilted her black eyes up at her owner.

However, Rory was taking no heed at all. He now made his way back out of the gateway, realising that the person inside was refusing to open the door. "Some people are so ignorant, not answering the doorbell. It's unbelievable!" he yelled. He then placed his hand back under his dark clothing.

Adam could feel sweat build up inside his mask and blur his vision. He had had enough of Rory's company and was vexed at not having been paired off with Paul. He clenched his fists tightly together. His instinct told him that things weren't going to get better anytime soon.

Noticing a spray can of some sort make its way into the palm of Rory's right hand, he feared the worst. Rory raised and shook the can before shooting a slimy substance out from its top.

"What are you doing?" hollered Adam once again, pulling his mask off to get a closer look.

Rory was waving his wrist up and down as he vandalised the outside wall with a sort of gory, sticky glue that he had obviously got in some joke shop.

"It's Halloween, we have to leave our mark!" Rory replied. He smirked from ear to ear, reached for some more chewy sweets and fled the scene of the crime.

Club eased her way closer to the bright green slime that was now foaming up as it mixed with the oxygen in the air. She began sniffing it, but quickly pulling her head back. She sneezed violently several times.

Adam stood in disbelief. He didn't know what to say. He nervously checked over his shoulder to see if anyone had come to the door, before leaving the property. Then he followed Rory back towards their house.

Adam walked slowly behind, not wanting to be

close to such an inconsiderate individual. He hadn't even invited this boy over, and after being so kind and allowing him to stay – this was the gratitude he showed him! It was no wonder he had no other friends.

He dragged his feet. They felt heavy. Then Rory suddenly turned around. It seemed like he had heard something from behind. Adam looked down the road and saw a group of people gathering on the footpath. Soon another gang, also wearing masks, gathered and began walking down the road.

"They look like boys in our class, let's see where they're going. Come on, Adam!" cried Rory excitedly. He grabbed some more sugary sweets. Before Adam could reply, Rory was off down the road. Adam thought about going back to his own house but decided instead to check out where everyone was going.

As Rory came closer to the youngsters, he waved his hand up and down. Adam noticed some familiar faces, but they were painted in all sorts of colours. It was some of the Adam's friends from school, along with several girls from the town.

"Hey guys, come on! The party has started, let's go!" a boy's voice shouted from under a mask.

Rory looked at Adam. Adam now understood where the group were going. It was the Halloween Party at the Fogs' house that was the big attraction.

"Come on Adam, let's check it out, we're invited," cried Rory. He shoved his bag of treats into his pocket.

Adam looked confused. He had practically forgotten about the party. But he knew he wasn't allowed to go. He looked around and started to weigh up his options. So far the night with Rory was going very badly. Some excitement might be just what he needed. He scanned the area to see if Jack or Paul were in sight.

In two minds, Adam beckoned Club to follow close by as he joined Rory and the group in their walk to the Fogs' house.

After a rather long walk, Adam could hear loud music coming from a large house just up ahead. Club perked up her ears, listening to the screams and chatter reverberating down the road. As the gang drew nearer, it was evident that this was an open-invite party. There must have been a hundred young people outside the house, with the clear sounds of what seemed like another hundred inside. Rory broke away from Adam and joined the gang as they made their way through the multitude of boys and girls in Halloween costumes out on the Fogs' front lawn.

The lawn was surprisingly big, and surrounded by neatly trimmed bushes. Children were dressed up as werewolves, goblins and pumpkins, while some others had chosen the comical side of Halloween and dressed up as celebrities. Adam couldn't recognise anybody but was getting the impression, judging by their size, that most of the young people here were much older than him. Some looked like they were in their late teens.

Keeping Club close by him, he walked indoors to try and find some of his fifth-class friends. Just like his own house, the Fogs' home was decorated with Halloween props that completely dominated the walls and ceilings. In the hallway Adam noticed a group of boys playing a game of blind man's bluff, where one person was blindfolded and had to tag the other children who ran around. Immediately Adam got the sense this game was been taken to another level as the children that ran about kept throwing things at the boy who was blindfolded while jeering and laughing in his direction. It didn't seem fun at all for the blindfolded boy and appeared more like a form of bullying.

In the dining room, music roared out from a sound system that was set up beside the couch. Girls danced about holding drinks in their hands while others picked from the selection of burgers and chips that lay on the tables. In this room a lot of people had their Halloween masks off so Adam could recognise some of them. He soon identified Terry, an older boy from Willows Town who sometimes stopped in the town to admire Club when Adam brought her for a walk with his Dad. Terry was a very popular boy in the town and most of the younger children liked to be around him. Adam took off his mask when he noticed Terry peering over in his direction.

"Adam, Happy Halloween!" shouted Terry over

the loud music, visibly high from the sugary drinks or other beverages that were being passed around.

"Come on outside, we're messing around. We'll show you what we have been doing all evening," he cried. Terry bent down and patted Club on the head several times before beckoning Adam to join him at the back of the Fogs' house.

As Adam walked out towards the back of the house, he scanned the area to see if there were any parents or other adults floating about, but couldn't see any signs of this party being supervised.

Here there was a tarmacadam area – then a spacious back lawn. More teenagers scampered around, seemingly out of control. They were jumping up and down on a trampoline laid out on the grass, or spraying colourful dye on some surrounding walls. Adam wasn't feeling at all comfortable. He wanted to go back to his own party, at his house.

Adam and Terry were joined by William, who pulled out a brown bag from under his jacket. William opened the bag and inside was a range of fireworks. Instantly Adam looked up at Terry, wondering if he was just showing him these or whether he had some plans for them.

William took a firework from the bag and reached for a cigarette lighter inside his upper pocket. Adam stood back but tried not to act scared in front of the older boys. William lit the end of the firework's fuse and held it in his hand as it began to burn.

Crazily, he left the firework in his hand for several seconds before throwing it up the back garden, not far from where a group of girls were chatting.

Scrrrrreeeeeeecch! went the firework. It darted to and fro on the grass like a snake before crashing into a flowerpot and exploding with a devastating *Boooooooooom!*

Club leaped back, frightened by the noise, and the girls close by screamed and jumped.

Adam stood still in disbelief.

What William had done was very dangerous. But he didn't seem to care. Fidgety, just like Terry, he reached for another firework, this time a larger one. He pulled over one of the refuse bins, he lit the firework's fuse and popped it inside the plastic bin. He slid the bin over to where some older teenagers were smoking in the corner and dancing to very loud music. Seconds later the bin lifted from the ground with a bang, and the teenagers scampered frantically away. Terry and William laughed and laughed as they reached for the bag, yet again.

Adam was feeling more and more uneasy. He couldn't believe how foolish these boys were and what risks they were taking. He looked around nervously, wondering where Rory was so he could head back to his own house.

"Here Adam, have a go," said Terry, handing Adam a long firework from the bag. Adam breathed out heavily, unsure what he should do. But before he could make up his mind, Terry had forced the firework into Adam's hand and passed him the lighter. Club gaped up at Adam as if she was trying to tell him not to do it, but Adam felt he couldn't show weakness in front of these older boys. He took the lighter warily and flicked back the top to generate the spark. Holding the firework in his left hand, he looked for a safe place to throw it. Then he lit it and aimed for the ditch.

As he aimed, Terry grabbed the firework off him and tossed it in towards the back door of the house.

Boooooooooooooommm! went the firework, and smoke filled the air. Party-goers dashed out in the mayhem. There was suddenly a silence.

The music from inside and outside the house stopped. The firework had clearly made its way through the back door of the house. Lots of children were just inside that door.

Adam's heart skipped a beat.

Looking around, he realised that Terry and William had disappeared. They had fled the scene. Boys and girls now stopped and stared in Adam's direction. Frightened of getting into serious trouble for something he hadn't done, he sprinted away towards the front of the house. He didn't dare turn around and see what had happened.

Club galloped behind as the two flew past the groups of children. Then they saw Rory out on the roadway.

"Come on, Rory, I'm going home!" shouted Adam. He checked over his shoulder for anyone looking for him.

Rory held his mask by his side and stared back in at the house.

"Did you hear that?" he said.

But Adam wasn't hanging around. He was already racing down the road with his mask back on, Club chasing behind him.

Chapter 4 –Adam's Headache

Along the way Rory explained how he and a group of sixth-class children had been down the road egging some houses. There were streams of egg yolk, rotten kiwis and mandarins stuck to his coat as he recounted the many houses that had felt the wrath of his powerful throw. Adam shook his head in disapproval, but he knew that his own behaviour hadn't been at all good. He realised that someone could be seriously hurt back in the house.

Just as Adam was thinking about going back to the Fogs' house to put his mind at rest, he heard a frightening roar from behind, and Rory came to an abrupt stop. Adam looked around and caught sight of a big, shadowy figure coming in their direction. The figure appeared to be wearing a Halloween mask. Rory had to look twice as the face looked uncannily human. The person had long frizzly hair and was wearing a wide-open black coat like something a magician would wear.

Rory stopped his fast-paced chewing and stood still as a statue.

"What – is – that?!" he cried out nervously, moving back to Adam and tapping his shoulder. "Who do you think that is dressed up?"

"Is that someone's actual face?" replied Adam, puzzled.

As soon as Adam went to take off his mask for a better look, the being advanced rapidly towards them making a sound like it was possessed. Adam's heart began to pump faster and faster. Was this someone from the house where Adam had thrown the firework? Or was it the man who hadn't come to the door earlier and who now had seen his wall vandalised with gooey Halloween spray?

He didn't want to wait to find out.

Without delay, he signalled Rory to start running back home as quick as possible. Rory didn't need to be asked twice. Clutching the bag of treats, he raced down the street. Club, seeing everyone running, thought the boys were playing a game of catch and darted off, soon leading the way.

The boys began to up their pace, both trying not to let their heavy outfits and accessories hold them back, but the person following them was moving even faster. They could hear the sounds of footsteps closing in on them, and a disturbing voice filled the cold air.

As Rory approached Adam's house, he dropped his bag of goodies. He leapt over the wall and dashed up to knock on the front door. By the look on his face he would do anything just to get inside. Adam was now up beside him waiting desperately for his Mum or Dad to let them in, knocking harder and harder.

The strange person sprinted into the driveway after them with its hands moving in all directions like a zombie. Adam pushed madly at the door handle and Rory began to scream.

"Come on, Club! Attack, attack!!" cried Adam, fearing the worst.

But Club didn't obey. She began to wag her tail and sprinted up to the dark figure. Seconds later a familiar voice was heard.

"Haha! I got the two of you!" said Dad, laughing at the top of his lungs.

Adam and Rory, still petrified, pulled their

hands from their faces to look at who it was. Dad took off the long-haired mask.

"I got this at the auction. It's a good one, isn't it?" he panted.

Adam and Rory stood in shock as they gathered their thoughts and emotions, not knowing what to say. Adam felt a little embarrassed that he had gotten so scared in front of Rory. Rory, who still did not look at all well, heaved a sigh of relief out onto the cold air. He pulled off his own mask, revealing trails of sweat running down the sides of his cheeks and a slick of hair along the top of his forehead.

"Ah yes, we kind of knew it was you alright," said Rory, catching his breath as he walked casually into the house. He totally forgot about the bag of treats he had dropped out by the front wall, but Jack and Paul were soon on the scene to discover the pleasant surprise.

Within minutes Rory had forgotten about the shock he had just experienced and gotten back to being his usual self. Inside the kitchen, Mum had laid out a plate of hot food for each of the boys. On each plate were some hot sausage rolls, chips and delicious pieces of crispy chicken. Jack poured out all the sweets and chocolate bars onto the side table. Some money also clattered against the wooden board, a sound always nice to hear. Club, who had sneaked in from the front door in amongst the commotion, licked her lips. She sat politely down by one of the chairs and waited for a portion of hot chicken to make its way down to ground level. The boys had to admit it all looked very appetising and the hot food was exactly what they needed after coming in from the bitter cold.

"Let's get this party started!" announced Jack as he pulled his seat out to make himself comfortable.

Rory began devouring as many portions as he could manage. It was almost as if he was eating as quickly as he could in case anyone asked him for something on his plate. Adam gazed over at him, wondering how someone could be so lacking in manners. Every so often Rory went towards the fridge to get the lemonade bottle for a refill. Mum was a little taken aback at how rude he could be when he burped after chugging down a full glass in one go.

"Right, would you like anything else, boys?" she asked. She looked sternly at Rory and got all the fizzy drinks and placed them out of reach.

"That's grand, thanks Mum!" Adam replied. Rory was too busy eating the chewy sweets to utter a word.

Adam left the table, unable to eat all his food, and headed up to his room. He needed a few moments' quiet to run over things in his head and think about whether or not he should tell his Mum or Dad about tossing that firework earlier. He felt something soft rub the inside of his leg as he walked up the stairs and noticed Diamond had followed him. Maybe she too needed a moment's rest from all the commotion of Halloween night.

Adam laid himself on his bed and raised Diamond up with his two hands. She felt warm and her legs dangled either side as she stared at Adam. Looking directly into Diamond's eyes, Adam could see his reflection. Immediately he began to see himself holding a firework in his hand and throwing it towards some children. He could hear the sound of the screech and boom in his head as it landed. Then he began to see Rory holding rotten eggs in his malevolent hands and firing them carelessly over house windows and doors. He reflected on all that sticky goo that had been sprayed over the house just down the road that would no doubt have hardened by now in the cold air.

"Ouch!" Adam snapped out of his daydream as he felt a nasty scratch on his right hand. He had obviously squeezed Diamond too tightly without realising it. He dropped Diamond and looked at his hand to see if there was any blood. Luckily it was only a scratch. Adam lifted himself back up off his bed and heard Rory laughing and chatting loudly in the kitchen. He had had enough of hearing his voice. It kept making him think about all the bad things that had happened. He took a few deep breaths and headed back downstairs to get Jack's attention so they could go out and cover some more houses.

He reached for his mask and made eye contact with his brother, hinting that he should join him outside. Jack, understanding the situation, pulled his hairy mask over his head once again and darted for the door to accompany Adam. He was eager to add to his stash of sweets and even make the ten-euro mark. Adam could see Rory was in the sitting room with Paul watching a horror movie – to the displeasure of Mum.

"Come on, Jack, we'll leave Paul here as well. We'll just go on our own."

"Make sure you stay nearby and only go to one or two more houses," said Mum, noticing the boys making their way out of the front door. "It's getting very late."

It had gotten even chillier outside and most of the trick-or-treaters had returned to their homes. The boys left Club behind in case she ran off after a stray cat. This late at night they planned on sticking close by each other. The two brothers set off up the road once again.

"It's so annoying going around with Rory. You should have seen what he did earlier. He sprayed this thick green spray all over someone's house just because they wouldn't come to the door," said Adam.

"Really? I told you he was a loose cannon. Cannot trust that lad," commented Jack. "I hope it wasn't Mr Boland's house. I hear he's gotten very sick lately. I think he had a heart attack or something and is spending his time in his bed recovering."

Adam frowned in thought. Maybe that was Mr Boland's house. That would explain why he didn't come to the door. He began to feel even worse at the thought of him seeing the destruction Rory had left on his wall. His night was getting worse and worse.

As they walked on the loose stones Jack noticed the Hidden House up the road.

Chapter 5 – Home!

"Come on, the Hidden House is just up ahead," said Jack edging forward with interest. "We have to check it out."

The reason the boys called it the Hidden House was because nobody could ever see the house from the road. It was completely concealed by a cluster of trees that stretched towards the sky. There was also a very long driveway into the house and it was a mystery as to who lived inside. It had been for sale for the past year and neither Jack nor Adam knew if anybody had bought it and was living there.

"We should go in and see if there is someone there," said Jack, his two beady eyes staring up the laneway. "They might be rich," he added eagerly.

Adam agreed. He felt a little nervous entering an unknown property but the fact that it was nearby made him feel a little more secure.

As the two walked cautiously up the driveway, little yellow lights came on beside them. They could also see a timber sign next to the path, which read 'Home'. The boys realised that the lights were automatically activated by motion sensors on the path. The lights made them feel safer; now they could sort of see where they were going.

The trees towered all around them, and they could hear one or two night creatures moving about in the tall, cold branches.

As they came closer to the house the boys were drawn towards three little lights that were shining from a small window towards the back. There were no cars parked outside, nor were there any signs of life. Adam noticed a large door at the front with an oversized door knocker. The brothers walked up to it cagily. They contemplated taking off their masks for a proper look around. Jack lifted up the knocker and let it drop on the door. There was a hollow thud. He waited for a few moments and then lifted the knocker to try one more time.

"There doesn't seem to be anyone at home," Adam whispered. He was almost relieved, now that he realised that any maniac could have come to the door. He stepped away towards the drive.

"Wait, wait a few seconds. There are lights on, which means somebody must have bought the house. They could be in there. Just wait a minute," said Jack.

Just as Jack was about to follow Adam out, they both heard long bolts being gently slid across from the inside. Adam turned back to see the door being eased open. Two small eyes gaped out.

"Who is it?" a woman's voice called out from behind the door.

She was still in the dark and Adam's chest was pounding.

"Trick or treat! Trick or treat!" stuttered Jack, slightly in shock that there was someone at home.

The door eased inwards and a very elderly woman was to be seen. It was difficult to see clearly due to the lack of light but both boys peered through their masks to get a good look at her. The woman looked at least seventy years of age and had long grey hair reaching down to

her shoulders. She was rather small and her eyes appeared quite dead and sad. Her skin was saggy and the clothes she was wearing were tattered and ragged. She held the frame of the door and stared at the two Halloween masks in confusion. For a brief moment the thought passed through Jack's head that this could be anyone dressed up as an old woman, but when he looked closely at the woman's eyes he knew this was no costume.

"Um, were just going around doing some trick-or-treating, so we just said we would pop by," said Adam. He began to realise that this woman might not know what night of the year it was and might be frightened of their appearances.

The old lady gave a slight smile, and asked them where they came from. Jack and Adam noticed that her eyes tightened together as she bent over to take a closer look at the two visitors.

Jack, who usually just pretended he was from a different town or village, told the woman that they were from the neighbourhood.

The old lady waved her skinny hand to invite the boys into the house, and promised to find some treats for them. Her voice had a croaking sound to it, much like you would hear from a small frog.

The boys hesitated.

"We'll just wait here, thanks!" replied Adam. This woman was a stranger to them and they did not know anything about her. He didn't want to just walk into her house.

"No! No, my dears! It's too cold outside tonight. Come on in and I will have a look for something nice for the two of you," she insisted. She held the door open for the two boys to enter.

Adam again paused for a brief second, relying on his instinct to guide him down the right path. Reluctantly he and his brother stepped into the dark house and followed the elderly woman slowly down the hallway.

There was a smell of damp inside. No radiators seemed to be on. Jack hissed to Adam that it was colder inside the house than it ever was standing outside.

They edged their way down the carpeted hallway to the kitchen. A few lit candles allowed them to see some of the furniture and fittings. There were numerous religious pictures on the walls, including one large statue of the holy mother.

As Adam tiptoed through the glass-paned kitchen door, he was met by a scary-looking cat, who hissed angrily at the two masked faces. The cat screeched, eyes beading with vicious intent, and its claws stuck out through its paws. Adam jumped back in fright. Jack stood still, waiting for the creature to calm down.

The old lady apologised for her cat, explaining that it was not used to company and often got protective of its territory, just like a dog. As the woman spoke she clutched the sides of the kitchen sink to keep her balance.

"I can see that!" replied Jack, keeping his distance from the scruffy creature. The cat was very thin and had vivid green eyes which seemed to provide more light than the candles.

Inside there was an old-fashioned kitchen unit along with a run-down range that looked like it had been dormant for years. Hanging above it was a large clock, which had long golden chimes dangling downward. Jack and Adam had never seen such a strange clock.

"Sit down beside the table and I will find

something for you boys to eat," said the woman. She made her way into a side room.

Jack sat down on one of the old wooden chairs near a round table. He looked around at the home of the strange woman. Adam sat beside his brother and pulled off his mask to have a proper inspection. Jack was disinclined to remove his hairy-headed mask as it was almost keeping him warm in the cold damp of the kitchen.

This place is dead, thought Adam. He felt very confused as to how somebody could live in a place as run down and decrepit as this.

"From the outside you would think this place would be very upper class," mumbled Jack, checking out the photo frames on top of the ancient cupboards.

There were icy tiles on the ground and old-fashioned wallpaper covering the walls. There was a bowl for the cat over towards the corner of the room, half full of old, sour milk.

"Yuk! The poor cat, no wonder it's on edge!" said Jack. He turned his head away in disgust.

The frail woman lurched back to the kitchen with her bitter-looking cat, who threw Jack a devilish eye from the distance. She placed a plate of biscuits on the table and poured out two large glasses of cold milk for the young boys to drink.

Jack and Adam immediately examined the condition of both the glasses and the biscuits. The glasses were dirty, with grime caught along the edges, while the biscuits looked like treats you wouldn't even throw a crowd of ducks. The milk, however, appeared nice and cold, and it drew the attention of the woman's cat.

"We are fine, thanks. We are just after eating back home," explained Adam truthfully.

The woman insisted that they eat and drink, edging the plate of old soft biscuits closer towards them. Her voice croaked even more in persuasion. She could now see the faces of both Adam and Jack, as Jack had felt it a little rude to keep his mask on while at the table. The woman pulled up a small stool and slowly reached for her spectacles so she could see the children better.

She eyed up each of the boys in turn and then licked her dry lips.

"You are fine young boys. What are your

names?" she asked. She settled in her chair and awaited a reply.

Adam hesitated for a brief moment.

"I'm Adam, and this is my brother, Jack. What is your name?" Adam asked, throwing the conversation back on the woman. He didn't want to disclose too much information about himself and his brother.

There was a brief pause.

"I'm Dorothy Childers. I moved here from the city after my husband died twelve months ago," she said softly.

Adam could detect small tears forming in her eyes as she thought about her dead husband.

Chapter 6 – Hooligans

"I haven't been in this house long. My husband – he died on this night, the thirty-first of October last year, after he was attacked coming home from the pub," she said quietly. "There were too many memories in our old house, so I had to move."

The woman stared into space as she told her story. The scruffy cat, sitting up on her long grey skirt, purred as she stroked it firmly up and down to hold back the tears.

"My husband Alfred was just minding his business when a group of hooligans messing about on Halloween night thought it would be funny to pounce on him and beat him up," said the woman. "He was a very mild man, not a troublemaker," she added, shaking her grey head in dismay.

She went on to explain that he had just finished a work project that night and decided he would head out for a few drinks with some of his colleagues. The police had described the attack as one of "malice and of tragic circumstances".

"It was a very dark night, like tonight," she said, "when that group of young people took my poor husband from me."

Adam and Jack were feeling more and more uncomfortable. They were only young children; they did not know how to react to this old woman's pain. They weren't sure if they should say something or just stay silent. Adam had seen from films that in situations like these the person might need a gentle hug to get the strength needed, but realised he was still talking to a stranger, and banished the thought from his head.

"Is it OK if I use the bathroom?" asked Jack. He needed to stretch his legs, and was also feeling somewhat intimidated by Mrs Childers' cat, who was eyeing him up and down.

"Yes, my dear, it's upstairs on the left," answered the woman using her skinny finger to point up the stairs.

Jack left his mask on his chair and walked up the creaking stairs. He could see lots of doors in

front of him and wondered where each of them would bring him. The woman was still chatting downstairs, and he didn't want to leave Adam too long on his own, so he decided just to go to the toilet and stop being nosy.

As Jack walked in the bathroom door he was stopped in his path by something soft that shot straight into the back of his mouth. Jack spat, trying to clear his throat. He looked up and realised he had walked into a large cobweb that covered most of the doorway.

Looking down the sides of his Halloween costume, he saw that it had gotten all over his clothes.

Using his hands, he flicked at the cobweb hanging from the door and cleared it all out of the way so he could pass through. He entered the bathroom, and immediately regretted it. Some maggots were crawling around the toilet bowl, while spiders sat on other large webs along the walls. Jack held his breath, flicked more cobweb from his hair, and decided to go back down and join his brother.

Downstairs Adam seemed like all the chatter was draining the life from him. He sat nodding as the woman talked more and more about her life. Jack sat down and pretended to drink from the glass.

By the manner in which the woman was going on, Adam and Jack realised that she was probably not as old as they had initially presumed. The stress and hardship of the last year had obviously had an ageing effect on her. Her lips were dry and her mouth sunken.

"I got this cat after his death, to keep me company. I haven't been able to think of a name yet," she croaked. She then began rubbing its soft skin to and fro on her lap.

"How about Weirdo?" whispered Jack. He smirked across to his brother, who struggled not to laugh.

All of a sudden the woman paused. She turned and directed her attention towards the large clock hanging over the range. She flicked the feline off her lap and got up from her chair hurriedly, showing more signs of life that she had before.

Jack and Adam could see it was approaching twelve o'clock.

"Please join me for a prayer. It's Alfred's

anniversary," said Mrs Childers.

The brothers knew it was certainly time they got back to their own house – their parents would be worrying – but they did not want to just run out and leave this woman after all she had told them.

"OK, we'll say a quick prayer and then we'd better be heading home," said Adam.

The three of them made their way through to a nearby bedroom, where three more candles were burning on a desk, around a picture of a man who must have been the husband. There was a selection of religious statues that seemed to form a small shrine by the bedside. The room felt so damp, Jack and Adam could almost hear the candles quenching.

"This must have been the light that we saw from outside," said Jack, nudging Adam on the shoulder.

Adam didn't even hear what he said. His mind was preoccupied with all that was going on. He didn't like where he was going. There could be a basement in here where the woman would trap him and his brother. Maybe this whole husband talk was just a ploy to get them to naively follow her. The hairs along his arms and legs stood on end.

Jack stared at the largest picture on the wall, which was a portrait of Mrs Childers and her husband on their wedding day. Mr Childers stood tall and happy alongside his wife. The woman knelt down on the ground in front of the picture and joined her skeleton-like hands around rosary beads to begin a prayer. Adam and Jack stood behind her and bowed their heads in respect. As she recited her short prayer, the noise of the big clock could be heard from the kitchen. It struck twelve o'clock. The chimes echoed, one after another, throughout the house.

Adam heard the door creak, and quickly lifted his head. His heart began to pump fast. He felt like someone else was there.

At once the candles went out in a puff of smoke. Jack looked up in confusion. The cat hissed as if it had detected something nearby. Adam and Jack stood still, breathing heavily in and out.

Then the candles flicked back on.

"What's going on?" Adam asked nervously, clutching the sides of his costume.

The widow was shaking furiously as she knelt in front of the picture, continuing to pray. Her eyes were closed and the rosary beads in her hand swayed to and fro. Jack came closer to his brother, freaked out at what was taking place. There was cold sweat on his forehead and his heart was racing.

The picture of the husband suddenly crashed to the ground as if it had been thrown. A silhouette of a man cast a shadow across the floor, and the room seemed to get colder.

Jack and Adam were rooted to the spot, staring at the silhouette. They were struck with an intense feeling of fear.

Instantly a gust of wind swept through the old damp house. The cat hissed at the gust as it passed by, its bright green eyes protruding from their sockets.

The woman now looked upwards and called out her husband's name over and over again. Her body shook as if she was having an epileptic fit.

"Alfred! Aaaalfred! Come back to me! Come back to me!" she cried intently.

Jack couldn't handle any more, but he found he

wasn't able to move. He looked across at his brother, whose body appeared to be vibrating. Jack realised there was something seriously wrong. He remembered hearing a priest once talk about how some people's bodies could become possessed. This room now felt like it was occupied by something supernatural. He needed to do something before it was too late.

He felt a surge of energy that gave him the courage to move. He shouted into Adam's face and then pushed him to the exit. Adam, in a panic, did his best to move his stiff legs to follow his brother.

The two boys stumbled towards the door down the hallway which, mysteriously, had been left completely open. The wind had increased outside and the trees swayed violently backwards and forwards. They bundled themselves out the door and ran back down the long driveway, triggering the automatic lights once again. They didn't stop for a single second. Both boys could hear the sounds of a siren in the distance. Their Halloween masks had fallen from their grasp but they were too petrified to even think about going back.

Chapter 7 – Principles of Loss

They didn't stop running until they reached their house and banged loudly on the door. Mum met them at the entrance with a look of anger on her face.

"Where were ye?" she cried. She noticed the frightened looks on her two sons' faces. "Why did you disobey me and go to the Fogs' party earlier, Adam? Rory's parents are just after coming over and taking Rory off home, he's in big trouble!"

Adam didn't hear a single thing. He was still in utter shock. He stared into space, not processing what his Mum was saying.

"Some girl has gotten injured because Rory stupidly threw a firework inside the door. She's gone to hospital with a cut on her arm. For everyone's sake, let's hope she's OK," said Mum, shaking her head in disgust.

Hearing the word "firework", Adam snapped

out of the trance he was in. He began to realise what his Mum was on about. Rory must have been blamed for throwing the firework at the Fogs' house earlier when it was he who was really responsible for it. Feeling sick to his stomach, he bowed his head and walked with Jack down to the kitchen to try and think. It was getting all too much for him.

Granny was seated inside the door with a cup of tea in one hand and a biscuit in the other. She had her right foot gently placed on Club's stomach. Club lay motionless like she had been knocked out in a fight. Granny did not seem to be doing anything, just staring and thinking, with a slight look of sadness on her face.

When she looked up she noticed the boys, both pale as ghosts and with haunted looks on their faces.

"Well, hello my boys, how did it go?" granny inquired, swallowing the last chunk of her biscuit.

Jack was first to speak. "We were in the house across the road, with the long driveway, and a woman was living there. The woman had a cat and she told us about her husband getting attacked and dying one year ago today," he recounted, trying to calm down. "And then we went in to say a prayer and all these weird things started happening. Candles were blown out, things started shaking and the old woman was acting as if she was possessed, and we saw something else... It was awful," he added.

Adam nodded his head. He was still thinking about what his Mum had just told him. Rory must have got in trouble for tossing the fireworks, maybe because of his reputation. Or maybe Harry and William said it was him because they knew he was always getting into trouble. He thought about owning up, but then remembered all the trouble Rory had nearly gotten him into tonight.

Granny pulled two stools out from the table to get the boys to sit down and tell her more. Jack flicked off his long jacket and filled two glasses of fizzy orange before handing one to his brother who had sat down. Gradually he and Adam began to feel a little more relaxed.

"There was this gust of wind also, and the cat even started to act strange," said Jack.

Granny looked very interested but did not

appear to be fazed by any of this talk. She gathered the two boys closer and stared into space for a few seconds before speaking.

"When you lose someone very close to you it can be extremely difficult. Sometimes it can be impossible to let them go. When your grandfather died a part of me died also. There is not a day that goes by that I do not miss or think about him."

Adam and Jack could see the sorrow in their granny's eyes.

"At Halloween they say some of the spirits of the past come out and give a sign to those they have left behind. Cats are believed to be able to see some of the spirits of the dead." Her eyes were closed as if she was trying to remember something. "Your grandfather has spoken to me several times in dreams that felt like real life. It can be so powerful."

Mum now entered the room and Adam kept his head down, not wanting to get into a big argument about disobeying her and going to the Fogs' house.

"These signs are sometimes a way of showing us that the people who have died are still looking over us and protecting us. Remember, when a person dies their body dies with them but their soul can still live on," Granny said.

She then pointed to the broach she was wearing on her cardigan. On it was a small cut-out picture of Granddad.

"I just touch this and ask for help sometimes when I am struggling," she explained. She bowed her head to give it a gentle kiss.

The two boys now felt much more at ease. They were still baffled at their experience but could now look at it in a different light. They knew they were very lucky to have their grandmother alive to share some knowledge only people that had lived a long life could disclose.

Jack slurped down his orange, which now was a little flat. Club woke up. Hearing the sound of drink or food, she perked up her ears and placed her paw on Jack's lap, asking for a treat.

Granny started to laugh, and slowly got off the stool to rub the top of Club's head. "It's a pity you couldn't see some of the ghosts, like your partner Diamond," she giggled. She stroked the smooth blond hair between Club's soft ears.

"Ha, well even if Diamond could, I don't think

she would be bothered!" Jack replied, before bursting out laughing just like his granny.

Hearing all the commotion, Dad entered the warm kitchen.

"So where are all the goods? Where did you two end up for the last while? You were gone so long it's November now," he said, reaching for a couple of leftover monkey nuts.

"We actually went across to the Hidden House, the one that has the timber sign with 'Home' on it," explained Jack. He felt somewhat uneasy talking about it.

"Yes, and some old woman lives there now," said Adam. "We won't be going back there again though. It was terrifying."

There was a pause as Dad chewed his monkey nuts.

"Some old woman? In the Hidden House? I don't think so," said Dad, looking confused. He sat down and made himself comfortable on one of the kitchen stools. He then reached for some more nuts from the packet.

"What do you mean?" asked Adam. He perked himself up and faced his father head on.

Dad finished his nuts and spoke.

"That property was put up for sale last year but nobody has occupied it since. I was asked to fix the interiors last week, and was over doing some measuring for new furniture a few days ago."

Jack and Adam tilted their heads towards each other. A sharp tingle made its way through each of their bodies.

The End

Jack and Adam's adventures continue in
'THE BLAZE'
Coming soon...

Books in *'The Adventures of Jack and Adam'* series

For more information on 'The adventures of Jack and Adam' series, please visit us on www.jackandadam.com

Also by Anthony Broderick
'The Larry Right' Series

eBooks now available in the Larry Right series

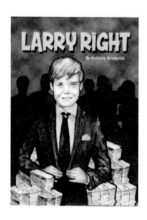 

For more information, please visit us on
www.larryright.com